CW00502327

Trigger warning

This book talks about death, abuse, domestic violence, sexually transmitted diseases and miscarriages.

Introduction

"Hello, everyone, and welcome back to this therapy group session. Last week, we heard from two of you ladies, but unfortunately, the rest of that session had to be stopped due to an unfortunate incident. So what we're going to do is carry on with last week's session. So, with that being said, is anyone willing to start us off?". Ms. Gates said. Ms. Gates is the group therapist for the women's correctional prison. Ms. Gates seemed nice. She reminded me of my great-aunt, Betty. They both were stubby little things with the most enormous back off you would ever see on anybody. In fact, she never had a backoff. She had a shelf attached to her back; that's how big her bottom was. She had a cute but mean face, with big bantu twists in her hair. I loved to see my black queens with their natural hair. Natural is the best, ladies.

"Summer, would you like to start us off?" she asked.

"Okay, yeah, umm. Hi, my name is Summer, and I have three years left to serve. I'm here because I decided to follow a man I thought was my life's love, but in the end, I saw him for what he truly was. He left me for dead and made me take all the blame for the robbery. I'm in a healing place right now, so I don't like to dwell on the negatives any more."

"Thank you, Summer, and I can see your progress since coming to the group. Well done." Said Ms Gates. "Right, now I want to hear from someone new to our group. Any takers?"

Everyone looked around to see who would be brave enough to speak out about why they were there. Looking around, I could tell everyone had a story, but like me, they were unwilling to bite the bullet and speak first. Hearing other people's stories gave me an escape from my tragic tale. Mine is not one I particularly want to talk about with anyone. But on the other hand, it could really help somebody someday. I think.

There was one woman there that kept staring at me. She was roughly 5'5/5'6 in height. She had long hair braided down to the middle of her back. She looked like Queen Latifa in the movie Set It Off, with braids like that. She looked like a solid size UK 18, but I could be wrong. She was pretty in the face for a bitch who has dry beef with me. Honestly, this woman has been dry-beefing with me since I got here. I remember the first day I arrived; she was one of the first faces I saw. And I kid you not, the bitch tried to fight me on my first day in prison. To this day, I still don't know the reason why she hates me. All I do is sit down, read my books, meditate and work. She hangs around a group of females that just give me bad vibes. The vibes reminded me of ' I'ma take your man' kind of bitch. Well, she could have mine. She might have to find him and dig him up first. I never knew her name, so I gave her one myself. Brenda. I don't know why, but she just looked like a Brenda.

I once knew a woman called Brenda, a beautiful woman with beautiful full lips, long flowing hair, and a body out of this world. The only thing I disliked about Brenda was that she was why my mother and father split up. Brenda was my babysitter when I was younger; she used to watch me while both of my parents used to go to work. Everyone in my household loved Brenda, especially my brother and father. One night, my parents were working late. I was meant to be in bed since it was after 8 o'clock, but this peculiar night, I could not sleep. I got up to find Brenda because I was having nightmares. I walked into the front room, and what I saw made my little heartbreak in two pieces. I had caught Brenda on top of my father. They were both naked as the day they were born. I screamed and ran into my bedroom; a few minutes later, my father came in, pretending everything was okay. I had told him what I had seen, but he told me it was all a really bad dream and kissed me good night. A few more weeks passed, and nothing had happened, well, so I thought. On my 9th birthday, it all hit the fan. My mom had caught my dad and Brenda in the back seat of her car. I will say that it was an eventful birthday as my mom beat up Brenda and my father. My mother kicked him out of the house, and I never saw him again until I was 10. My brother and I were walking through the aisle of Asda, and I saw my father with Brenda and what looked like a newborn baby. We ran home and told our mother, and she just sat there and cried her eyes out. From that day, I knew that all men are trash and they only think of themselves.

"Kenya, would you like to start us off?". Asked Ms. Gates, who had startled me out of my memory.

I stood up, dreading what was going to come of this.

"Okay then. Hi, my name is Kenya, and I'm here for killing my husband".

Chapter 1

1 ½ years ago

"Bitch you been fucking around on me?" screamed my husband. "Huh bitch?"

"No baby, why would I do that?" I said with a tremble in my voice. I hated when he would get in these types of moods. My husband Mike never used to be like this. There was a time when he used to adore the ground I walked on. There was a time when he used to call me beautiful and every lovely name you could think of, but these days, he bestowed every name to me apart from the name my mother gave me at birth.

Mike was a handsome-looking name, with light caramel skin and light blue eyes, and yes, they were his natural eyes. This was the first time I had seen something like it. They were so mesmerising. I used to get lost in them. But now, all I saw were the eyes of the devil staring back at me. I swear his whole face would contort into a demon-looking thing when he would get in these moods. Mike was a heavy drinker, but looking on the outside, you would never suspect that he was a heavy drinker. On the outside, he was a hard-working man who worked for

Jackson & Jackson Solicitors Limited. He was a big-shot lawyer who won all his cases. Everyone wanted him. We met at college and became college sweethearts; it was true love. Well, at least for me, it was.

Mike was a fan of the ladies; even the ladies in my family seemed charmed by him. He would also influence some men, apart from my brother Lance, in my family. Lance was two years older than me. But if we stood next to each other, many people assumed we were twins. That's just how much we looked alike. Lance hated Mike from the first time he met him; he used to say, 'Kenny, he reminds me of Pops' or 'he's going to do to you what Pops did to Mom'. But I kept telling him that he was being silly and would never do that to me. But guess what he did and much worse.

Mike won over my mother as soon as she saw him. He could never do anything wrong in her eyes. To her, he was what every woman wanted in a man, including her. Sometimes, the way she talks about him, she would have tried to find him before I did for herself. To my mother, he was everything; I had caught my mother looking at him a time or two when we used to go on family holidays to Jamaica. I could not blame her in a way because he was built like a God with muscles on top of muscles. I always wondered what drew him to me since I was a plus-size beauty. As they would say in Jamaica, I was fluffy. Not many men loved plus-size women, but Mike did, and when I say plus size, I mean I was a solid 16, but over time, I put on weight and became heavier. I became a size 24.

Smack

"Don't lie to me bitch, I just got back from the doctors, and they told me I have chlamydia and gonorrhoea. And it never came from me, so the only other explanation is you!"

Mike foamed at the mouth.

Chlamydia? Gonorrhoea?

Did this man just say he has chlamydia anddd gonorrhoea? Oh my god, does that mean I have chlamydia now? What the fuck is going on.

"Mike, stoppp, please! I've not cheated on you. I don't know how you got it. Please stop hitting me". I cried out in pain. Mike would come home in a rage every other month, spewing these heinous crimes. Crimes that I have not committed, crimes that we both knew he had done. But insisted on blaming me.

"You fat bitch, you out there fucking around on me. Huh bitch? Every time I give you a pass, and we get to a good place, here you go and fuck it up. I don't even know why I'm with you anymore. You're fat, ugly, can't cook or clean, and the pussy is trash. I should leave you and find someone better, somebody like the receptionist or maybe I should leave you for your mother. We both know she can cook better than you, plus she is sexy as fuck as well. Is that what you want, huh? You want me to leave you for somebody else?"

"N n nooo Mike, I'm ssss sorry I I I should not have stepped out o o of our marriage."

I know you're thinking, why am I blaming him for catching an STI. Trust me, it's easier to comply than reform. All the fight I once had has now gone out of my body. I'm tired of beating a dead horse. I've concluded that there was no way out for me. Nobody was coming to save me. I was in this alone.
I had gotten up from the corner I was crouched in and went to the bathroom. I left Mike downstairs clutching a cold beer; I travelled to the bathroom to clean myself up. Upon looking in the mirror, I saw that Mike had made a mess of my face; this time, makeup could not clear this up. I could tell by how my nose was leaning to one side that it was broken; I've come accustomed to knowing

when something on my body is broken now. I've had four broken bones: wrist, ankle, thumb and rib. A dislocated shoulder, sprained ankle and numerous black eyes. I was not new to this.

Looking at my nose, I knew this would be another hospital trip, but this time would be different since I was carrying his baby. I could not turn up at the hospital with a broken nose; the police and everybody else would be on our case, and I could not have that. So I got a towel, bunched it up in my mouth, took three deep breaths, and snapped my nose back into place.

"Argghhhhh!"

Thank God for my muffled screams.

Hot tears were rolling down my face; my nose was throbbing like a heartbeat. Blood flowed down as though it was a waterfall. My nose had taken on a purpley colour. I just knew it would stay like this for a few weeks.
I walked out of our bathroom, contemplating what life was. Is this really the life I wanted for myself? I knew God did not plan this for my life. Laying down on our bed, I tried to forget about my pain, but the pulsating sensation in my head kept me from falling asleep.

"Here, take these fucking pills. I got them from the doctor when they told me I caught chlamydia and gonorrhoea from you," He said while throwing a bottle of antibiotics at me. "I got enough for both you and me."
I lay still, trying to block him out.

"While you are laying there, you better not take your ass to work tomorrow, with the way your face is fucked up. You lucky I got that contact that can sign you a fake doctor's note letting your boss know you're off sick for a few weeks."

Ring ring

"Hello..... Yeah..... OK, I'll be there in a bit. Let me just finish up here...... Oh yeah, I told her...... Nah, she is not gonna be a problem.... You know I got you, and I can handle that..... OK, I'll see you in a bit. Let me just wash up, and I'll be on my way... OK bye." He said while walking into the bathroom.
Who was he talking to?

Twenty minutes later, Mike walked out of the bathroom with a towel wrapped around his waist, steam flowing off his body. I felt the heat come out of the bathroom, and I thought that that water should have burnt his dick off and melted his body. Unfortunately, that did not happen. I watched him get dressed and wondered where he was going. If I asked him where he was going, would he kick off again? Lord knows I can't take any more beatings tonight. Fuck it, I'm going to ask.

"Umm, hunny, where are you off to?"

He looked at me like I was asking him a question; it was the stupidest thing that could come out of my mouth.

"Don't worry about where I'm going; just remember what you must do before bed. Email, text, call your boss and let them know you won't be in for a few weeks. I'll be back sometime tomorrow, and don't wait up for me." He said while bending down to my ear. "And since you never cooked, I'm going to find a bitch who will. Plus, I bet her pussy's tighter, and she is not a fat bitch like you," He whispered harshly in my ear.

And with that, he got dressed and left. Leaving me alone for another night, debating whether I should end it all and be done with this torment I call life.

Chapter 2

"Did you tell him yet?"

"No, not yet," I said while shaking my head.

"Come on, Kenya, you know you can't keep this hidden. He's going to find out sooner or later."

"I'll choose later. But for now, can we just keep this to ourselves. I'm not ready for him to know."

"Are you serious right now! Kenya, you're 4 months pregnant with my baby. Do you think I'm just going to let you continue this facade? Just look at your face. He could have killed my seed. If you don't send off those divorce papers today, it will be a problem," said Jason.

Jason was not only my colleague but also my step-brother-in-law. Jason's father had married Mike's mother when they were 15/16 years old. From what I've been told, they never got along in their teens. They were too different to get along; no matter how much they tried, they never seemed to gel well together. If you asked

Mike's mother, Shelia, she would describe them as the angel and the devil who sit on your shoulders. She said that Mike used to be a devil until he went to college and met me, and Jason was an angel until he reached college and turned into a devil.

She seriously messed up her life because Mike was the devil himself.

I know messing around with my brother-in-law was not ideal, and getting pregnant was definitely not perfect, but shit happens. Jason and I's relationship came just at the right time. See, I was on the verge of killing myself. I had a plan; I wrote my letter and arranged all my affairs. I even had documents showing my medical history and all the bruises and broken bones I had sustained from Mike. I was sitting in my car, parked in the school parking lot, working late that night. I had a bottle of Hennessy that I was downing. I had already put a cloth ball in my exhaust pipe and had the car running. All I had to do now was wait until the carbon monoxide had seeped into me and filled my lungs with poison. I could feel the power of the alcohol and the fumes putting me to sleep. I had wished for death to take me peacefully. As I closed my eyes, I knew death had greeted me. Hello, my old friend. But death did not welcome me; death stood at the door and told me it was not my time.

I awakened to a bright light shining in my eyes. Is this heaven? I thought. But sadly, it was not. The beeping sounds and the white walls let me know I was in a hospital room. I had turned my head to the left when I saw Jason sitting beside my bed with tears in his eyes. I remember him asking me why, I was trying to kill myself. I basically told him it was because I was stuck. He told me he had found the note in my car with all the documents, but Mike had walked in before he could speak anymore. Mike came inside asking me a whole load of questions, and I could not answer him truthfully, so I just told him and the doctors that I just felt over-stressed with work. That excuse seemed to work, and the doctors sent me home 2 weeks later. I will say that when I reached Mike, he was a different person towards me; he was more attentive than he had been in a while. But that lasted 3 weeks, and then he returned to his wicked ways.

"Jason... you just don't understand," I pleaded.

"What don't I understand? Enlighten me. Because from where I'm standing, it's pretty easy to do." he said while sighing. "Look, I know the way we got together was not correct, and I'm stepping on my stepbrother's toes here and trust me, I'm going to hear the backlash from my parents about this, but I can't help how I feel. I fell in love with you, Kenya, and I won't apologise for loving you. I won't sit here while your stomach gets bigger and bigger and you are still with him. Either you do something about it, or I will!"

Hearing the passion in his voice, I could tell he was at the end of his rope with this situation. I understood where he was coming from because I was also at my end; the only thing stopping me from going the whole way was Mike. I love my husband; I love him to a certain extent, but am I in love with him? No, I'm not.

I kept thinking about all the hurt and pain I had gone through with being with Mike. All the bruises, broken body parts. And I can't forget about the miscarriages. This man caused me to suffer 5 miscarriages and 1 stillbirth. Touching my stomach, I started to think about my son that I lost; I remember it like it was yesterday; I remember the sheer pain that was coursing through my body when Mike pushed me down the stairs, and I hit every single step, the gushing feeling of my water breaking, the smell of iron in the air coming from the blood dripping out of my vagina. I remember him taking me to the hospital and repeating the exact words: 'Tell them you missed a step, remember that's how to fall, do you hear me?'. The pain of pushing my child out and watching the light go out in his eyes was one of the hardest things I had ever been through. As I was only 23 weeks old, they could do nothing to save him. I had to be 24 weeks pregnant for them to even try and save him, so I sat there and watched him fight for his life for an hour until his little lungs gave up. My little Prince.

"Kenya, Kenya! You don't hear me calling you? Are you ok?"

"Yes, sorry, I was just thinking, and I lost my train of thought. I umm.." I knew I had to pick my words carefully. If I said the wrong thing, this could blow up in my face. "Look, Jason, please give me a little more time. This is a delicate situation, and you know this. I just need time to get everything in order, and then we can be together, and I can be safe and happy."

I could see the look of defeat on his face. I knew this was not the answer he wanted to hear, but it was the only answer I could give him. My mind was running a hundred miles an hour, and I needed it to stop now; if not, I would surely pop.

Watching Jason walk away broke my heart as I knew it was not what we wanted to happen right now. I wanted to scream and say, 'No, don't leave; the divorce papers are already signed and ready to go,' but I could not say those words. I knew I was destined to be with Jason, but needed time to sort things out.

Chapter 3

A few days had passed since I last saw and spoke to Jason. I felt he was avoiding me because I still had lingering issues between Mike and me. Truth be told, Mike and I have been in some way getting along with each other, I have not received any black eyes or broken/ fractured bones, apart from the ones that are healing now. Mike even made me breakfast in bed this morning. I guess the only reason he's been being nice to me now is because he somehow found out that I was pregnant of course I know that it's not Mike's baby, and I know I should tell him but…… if I tell him…. let's just say that I would no longer be able to tell my story. So, I let him think I was carrying his child. Was it wrong of me? Yes, it is, but a bitch got to do anything to stay alive at this point.

Was I still in love with Mike? I don't know. All I know is that my heart still beats for him, and somewhere in my mind wants to make this work with him but I know it won't work in the end especially when he finds out that this is not his baby, and it actually Jason's baby. Wrapping my head around it all is giving me significant anxiety. I feel for Jason; I know this situation is not ideal, especially when we are at family events, and he has to watch his brother rub and kiss me and pretend we're happy. I fully knew that the day before, I would have cried to him about another bruise or broken body part.

What am I to do?

I have no one to talk to or express my feelings about it. If I were to speak my mind, everyone would give me the side eye cause I know I would.

Ding ding

I looked down at my phone and saw a notification pop up; it was a reminder that tonight was the school faculty party. I sighed, knowing that Jason would be in attendance.

I could tell Jason avoided me when we were at work together. I would see him in the halls or the staff room, and he would turn the other way; he's now fed up with this situation. Who could blame him? But guess what? Luck was on my side as I remembered that he would be sitting at our table when it was time to eat; the only problem would be... Mike...

Shit! I forgot that Mike will be attending with me. Fuck! It's just my luck to have the people I'm sleeping with sitting at the same table.

How did my life end up like this?

I had the most beautiful brown complexion, and my eyes set on my dreams. I had a plan for how I was going to navigate my life. But I let a man I thought loved unconditionally tear me down and belittle me. I let him take off the beautiful crown that was once placed on my head. I allowed him to throw it away in storage, never to be seen again. Never to breathe air, never to see the light of day. My crown was my life..... and I allowed him to let it shrivel and die.

I have become a former shell of myself and did not know how to bring her back. I missed who I was. In the famous words of Yovanna from Real Housewives Of Atlanta season 11, "I was that bitch. I was Yovanna from Clark", but instead of being Yovanna from Clark, I was Kenya from Newman University. I was a hot bitch on campus, but I still had my struggles. But I NEVER EVER let my crown slip until I met Mike.

"You ready? We got to be there by 7, and it's already half six?" Mike asked me

Shit, I forgot I was meant to be getting dressed. I quickly finished putting on my blue dress that helped conceal my pregnant belly. Not that you could tell I was pregnant anyway.

The journey to my work party was eerie but quick, as we lived only 20 minutes away from my workplace. The silence in the car was deafening. You could hear my heart beating out of my chest. **Bum, bum, bum bum.**

I was sweating like a sinner in church. I'm sure Mike caught on to the nervous energy I was producing as we walked into the building. I turned to look at him, and he had a perplexed look on his face.

"Why are you looking like that?" he asked.

"No reason. I'm just hot and out of breath."

"Fat bitch" I heard him mumble.

As we walked into the sports hall, I was impressed with the decorations they had put up. The school's sports hall had never looked better. Honestly, this was my second time this year coming in here. I used to love coming in here, but after we found a student hanging from the top uneven bar the gymnasts used, I could always feel her spirit whenever I entered. Tonight was no different. I often thought about Renè. She was a beautiful young girl inside and out and a great student, but she got in with the wrong group of people, and things turned terrible with her. She could not take the pain anymore and decided to end her life. I know how she felt since I tried to do the same thing, but I know now that that was wrong. Not that I did not know before, but I felt like I was left with no other option but to try and end it all.

Walking further inside, my stomach started to do a crazy amount of flips. I had a theory: whenever my baby knew their father was close by, they would go crazy. And tonight was no different. I looked to the left of me, and he was standing there, looking all handsome in his 3 piece blue attire; his blazer was the same colour, blue suede. We were matching tonight.

That fresh lineup and the waves he had in his head were spinning and making me seasick, and don't get me started on that beard. That glorious beard I loved to hold on to look perfect and well-greased.

God, this man was so fucking fine.

Just looking at him, I instantly got wet. Well, I hope it was my pussy getting wet and not me actually pissing on myself.

Trust me, ladies, it's happened before, and I'll save that for another story.

After an eternity, I finally stopped staring at him and approached the table.

While sitting in my seat, I looked at the menu, which read.

Starters
Halloumi, carrot & orange salad
Hot smoked salmon & beetroot platter

Mains
Spiced aubergine bake
Spinach & ricotta rotolo
Lamb chops with chilli & Ligurian broad bean pesto
Honey-glazed roast chicken & confit potatoes

Deserts
Retro trifle
Strawberry Cheesecake

My mouth started to water when I read what was on the menu.

Once everyone was seated, the servers came around and took each table's order. The conversation was friendly and light since nearly everybody at my table knew each other. Every so often, I would steal glances at Jason and catch him stealing glances at me; when I saw him looking, I would quickly look away and make sure Mike was not watching us.

Dancing in my seat, I was excited to taste my main course since my starter, the hot smoked salmon & beetroot platter, was so lovely that I wanted to lick the plate clean.

Inhaling the fumes of my dinner, my mouth watered with anticipation.

It was time for the main courses, and I could not wait to taste the honey-glazed roast chicken & confit potatoes. As the servers placed my meal in front of me, I inhaled the fantastic aromas from my plate. By the time I had blinked, my food was finished.

I started to have a sip of water when, from the corner of my eye, I noticed Jason staring at me with a sympathetic look. I quickly turned my face so it did not look like we were making eye contact, but I did not look away soon enough.

"Why does that nigga keep looking at you like that?" Mike aggressively whispered in my ear. "I don't know why he is looking at me," I replied with a treble in my throat.

Mike noticed the treble in my voice, and I could see the look on his face. And I knew this night was going to turn into a nightmare.

"The fuck you scared for?" Mike asked me, and then he turned to face Jason. "Why do you keep looking at my wife? What do you want her or something? It wouldn't be the 1st thing you wanted that was mine."

As soon as he said that, the whole room went silent. I could feel everybody's eyes on our table. I wanted to sink into my chair and crawl away, well, roll away with how big I was getting.

"Mike, what are you talking about? I wasn't staring at Kenya, but if you want me to look at her, then I will," Jason said while staring at me. I pleaded with Jason not to do this but knew I could not control his actions, so I knew this would not end well.

Before I knew it, Mike and Jason were wrapped around each other, throwing blows. Plates, food and drinks flew around like we were in a circus. Chaos was everywhere; I had nowhere to run to. I knew it was time to go when I saw about 3 people holding Mike and people holding Jason back. Looking at Mike, I could tell Jason got the better of him since one of his eyes was closed, and the other one looked like it was getting ready to close; his mouth and nose were leaking all over the place. I had to look away due to getting second-hand embarrassment. How do you start a fight and end up getting fucking up and losing the battle? What type of shit is that?

"LET ME GO!!" Mike yelled with spit spraying everywhere while managing to break free. "Kenya, bring your ass on and let's go!"

I could feel my baby kicking up a storm in my stomach. My anxiety was on a thousand, especially when everyone's eyes were on me. I wish walking out of the room was quick, but unfortunately, it was the opposite. Everything was moving at a snail's pace. I felt naked as everyone's eyes bore into my naked soul. With every step getting heavier and heavier, I needed to get out of there, so with everything in me, I started to run out. In the background, I could hear my name being called, but I could not turn around.

Making it out of the building, I saw Mike pacing back and forth from our car. Getting closer to the car, Mike stopped walking and gave me an evil blood-curdling stare.

"Get yo ass in this mother fucking car. Now." he gritted.

I dragged my feet towards the car. I knew it was a bad mistake to make as I knew this would be my last day on this earth. Saying a quick prayer, I got into the car.

Mike began speeding like a maniac, and other drivers were beeping their horns at us as we drove through multiple red lights, almost causing numerous car crashes. "You see what your hoe ass has caused now" Mike screamed at me.

"I never caused anything, Mike"

"Shut up bitch" SLAP! Mike backhanded me, and my head bounced off the passenger window. Instantly, my head started to bleed. At this point, I knew my body was like a fragile piece of art; one touch, and it would come tumbling down. "Fuck you mean you never caused anything? You think I'm blind?" SCREECH. Mike took a corner, and the car was almost on two wheels. "I have eyes bitch, that's why I dog you out the way I do. You're a fat hoe that must be treated just like a must. I can't stand the look of you; you're sloppy and out of shape. Not going to lie though the pussy is A1 still, but you can't even see it over that second body you are carrying around." Wait, did Mike know I was pregnant? That's impossible. "That's why I got a new bitch that's nothing like your ass, and guess what." Mike paused for dramatic effect. "She's *pregnant* with *my* baby."

Hearing what I heard, something took over my body; my body was on fire. I turned towards Mike, who had a smug look; I balled up my fist and punched him in his temple, which caused the car to swerve slightly.

"Oh bitch you've grown king kong balls now," Mike said while stretching his hands around my neck. Scratching at his hands, trying to get him off me, only made him squeeze harder.

Before we could react to what happened next, a car's bright, shining lights on the opposite side of the road were now in front of us. I screamed, but it was too late.

BEEEEEEEP, CRASH

It was too late, and everything turned black.

Chapter 4

Kenya in a coma

With the beautiful tropical breeze blowing against my skin, I knew I was in heaven. The beautiful clear blue sea and heat was my favourite part of this holiday; the warm sand between my toes felt glorious. I was loving life. Taking a sip of my virgin strawberry margarita, I smiled as I saw my children running around and playing in the sand.

"Luna, Star and Touissant play nicely with your sister, Willow baby; if they don't want to play with you, then play over there, ok."
"Ok, mommy, " said Willow. Willow was my baby. That little girl has been through so much for such a little person; she had open heart surgery at 5 years old, where they put a pacemaker inside of her chest, keeping her alive. She also has asthma. I swear my little princess had been through the wars, but she was a fighter.
My oldest child was Luna; Luna was my little Einstein; she was in the top class for everything. At 10 years old, the school gave her the year above homework, and this girl

was breezing through it all. Next was the twins at age 9 years old. Star and Touissant. They were the definition of Gemini people. The way these two could switch on someone would give you whiplash. Do something to one of them or their siblings, and you better sleep with one eye open. Trust me, I put them on punishment last time because they decided to rip all the paper wrapping on my tins, so I did not know what I was using. That was a sad day in the Steven's household.

"You baby that girl too much, Kenya."

"I do not," I said with a giggle while looking at my handsome husband, Jason.

"Come here," Jason said to me, and I got up and sat on his lap, "you know you are wearing the fuck out of this bikini" I started to blush; this man was always doing the most. "Let's put the kids the kids inside, and let's take a nap."

"A nap? Nigga you just want to fuck me again."

"So, that's what I'm meant to do as a husband, right?" He said while rubbing my booty.

"You acting like you can get me pregnant again." Yes, that's right, I was pregnant again. I was about to be a

mother of 5. I loved my life; everything in it was perfectly perfect.

BEEP BEEP

I looked down at the same time as my husband and saw he got a text message from his brother Mike. Mike was Jason's stepbrother since their parents married some years ago. Jason and Mike had a love-hate relationship towards each other; there was always this underlying feeling of animosity towards Jason. Mike seemed to always want his brother to fail. He made it factual that he wished for my marriage to fail. In his own words, "I give it 2 years before you fuck up and she leaves you", but the joke was on him because we had been married for 9 years, and everything was going great. I won't say it was a perfect marriage, as all marriages have trials and tribulations, but we managed to get through them. "Come on, baby, call the kids in so we can nap; you know I can't keep my hands off you," said Jason.

"Clearly, you can't. I'm on my 5th kid."

"Mann, my kids are a blessing, especially my boys; I can't wait til this little boy comes out of you. You hear that, little man, only a few more months left in there, and then it's me; you and Touissant are gonna roll out and have boy's

night; we gonna leave the girls to do the girl stuff," I giggled at his silly ass, and baby boy in my stomach was kicking up a storm agreeing with his father.

"Kids, come on, it's time to go inside now; I'm going to make dinner in 2 hours. Go have a shower to wash the sand off your body, and go and put on a movie; Daddy will make you some popcorn."

"YES, POPCORN!" my kids all screamed simultaneously. My kids are like me; we love some popcorn. The kids and my husband loved sweet and salted popcorn, while I loved salty popcorn with jalapenos. It sounds like a mad combo, but trust me, it works. It's like pineapple and pepperoni pizza; that shit is sooo fucking bomb, the sweet mixed with that salty taste, and if you add jalapenos to it, it gives the right amount of spice. It gives the chef's kisses. Gathering our stuff to go into our beach house, I turned to start walking when I heard a piercing scream come from Luna. I turned to see a look of horror across her face.

"MOM, YOU'RE BLEEDING, OMG YOU'RE BLEEDING!" Luna screamed.

"Mommy, why are you bleeding?" asked Willow

"Mom!" screamed the twins.

"My love, it's a lot of blood, fuck let me call the doctor; kids, help me help your mother inside and put her on the settee." My kids and husband carefully helped me into the house. At this point, I was so confused about what was going on at the moment. "Yes, I am still here; she's bleeding a lot....."

My vision was becoming blurry, and everyone's voices began to become entwined with each other. Until all I saw was darkness.

"Mommy, mommy, I am sorry, my time is up. I wish I had the chance to meet you, Daddy and my siblings," a voice called from the darkness.
I was so confused; what was going on? Who was this child, and why was he saying goodbye..? OMG, no, it can't be. Was this my baby boy? Omg, am I losing the baby? NOOOOOOO!!!!!

Before I could even open my mouth to answer him, a blinding light shot into my eyes, and I was transported into an area I did not recognise.

Chapter 5

Mike speaks

Everybody thinks I'm a gigantic asshole for everything you have seen, but you must understand everything I have been through.

I loved Kenya. I really did; I just could no longer be in love with her. When we first met, I loved everything about her: her skin, how she smelled, and everything. But what drew me the most was her smile. She was the first bbw I have ever felt attracted to, which blew my mind since I never found them attractive. LIKE AT ALL. I could never understand why somebody would want to be that weight and be happy and content with being big, but meeting Kenya changed my outlook.

I remember the day well it was the night my feelings towards Kenya started to change. We had just finished our 4th round of having sex, and Kenya was knocked out dead to the world, with slobber pouring out of her mouth with a pillow in between her legs. Kenya started moaning and laughing in her sleep, which was nothing new, but what followed after that was new to me. Kenya said a name which was not mine. Jason. Jason was the name she said, and my name is definitely not Jason.

Jason, mother fucking Jason.

My fucking stepbrother, this nigga has been a thorn in my side ever since he has been integrated within my family.

I hated this man even more now because of him. Kenya and I were in the hospital. I was leaving with just a broken arm, but Kenya, Kenya, was in a coma. FUCK!

There was a knock on the door, and I knew the detectives were coming to ask me more questions about the incident, so I pretended to be asleep.

Knock knock

"Mike, are you asleep?" said a voice I had become accustomed to love.

"Evelyn? Is that you?"

"Yes, my love", she said while moving towards my bedside. "Mike, what the fuck happened!?" she asked.

"I lost my cool and ended up fucking up that nigga and having an argument with Kenya in the car, and we ended up crashing the car."

She sighed

"Mike, first of all, is she dead? Because this can not work if she's dead."

"She's not dead; she's just in a coma, but I wish the bitch was dead."

"Hey, you can't say that here."

"Man fuck her, tell me how this bitch is pregnant, and I've not touched her in over 7 months?"

Eveyln's eyes ballooned just like mine when I found out that the doctor told me that Kenya was in a coma, but unfortunately, they could not save the baby. WHAT FUCKING BABY?

"So she was cheating on you?"

"Yeah, can you believe that shit" I scoffed "the nerve of that bitch. Who does she think she is? How she gone cheat on me? This bitch really cheated on me and ended up getting pregnant," I said more to myself.

"See, this proves everything we are doing is correct, and she deserves everything coming to her."

"I couldn't agree more."

"Yeah, especially when she finds out she's not the only one pregnant, and you plan on leaving her with nothing."

Before I could answer, there was a crackling sound, and I saw the door close. Who was that?

"Who was that?" I asked. Evelyn went and looked.

"It looked like your brother."

"I don't have a brother. But fuck do you think he heard anything? If he did, that might cause a problem for us." Fuck, if this bum ass nigga heard us, then he's going to be a problem.

I guess it's time to announce a service to the family.

Chapter 6

Jason speaks

After hearing what I had heard while walking past Mike's room, I started to speed walk towards the lift. I could hear my name being called and knew exactly who it was, but I continued walking.

 After getting on the lift, my mind was reeling from everything that had transpired this evening, from the fight with Mike to him and Kenya leaving the school and speeding off to me getting in my car to follow them as I could feel in my heart that something was going to happen to Kenya and my son, to me watching their car tumble twice in the air after colliding with the car on the other side of the road. I witnessed everything, and I was the one who called 999 while holding what looked like Kenya's lifeless body. Mike was in and out of consciousness as well.

After getting off the lift, I finally made it to my car. As soon as my ass hit the seat, I received a phone call.

"Sup pops?"

"Son"

"Yeah, pops."

"You need to make your way to the hospital. Mike and Kenya got in a car crash. Mike's okay, but Kenya's in a coma, and Mike is going to need all his family around him."

"I already know about the crash pops; I was the one who called the ambulance. I was in the car behind and witnessed everything."

"It's a good job you were there, hunny," I could hear my step-mom shout in the background.

"So, are you making your way there now?" he asked.

"Nah, I'm not. I don't think he wants me around him, especially after tonight's fight."

I could hear a scuffle, and then my mom's voice came louder on the phone.

"What do you mean you had a fight? What were you and Mike fighting about now? I swear you two will drive my blood pressure up sky-high again. I swear you two have been at it since you were little."

"Mmh"

"So tell me, what was it this time?"

"He accused me and Kenya of having an affair."

"What the hell? Well, we all know that's not true!" my pops and mom shouted.

Silence

My silence was deafening, and it was saying so much without me even opening my mouth.

"Jason, noooo, what the fuck was you thinking? Your brother's wife!"

"I knew that little hussy was up to no good; I can see now why Mike had been saying all those things about her."

Are they for real? I laughed at my parents because they both sounded excellent and dumb.

"Are you kidding, Pop how many times have you seen Kenya walk into this house with suspicious bruises or something is broken? And you, Mom, how many times has Kenya basically screamed in your face, asking for help.

Are you guys forgetting the time when she actually tried to kill herself? Don't forget I was the one who actually told you she tried to kill herself since I was the one who found the note and told you guys, and she begged me not to tell anyone. I know you guys can't be that blind and not see that Mike was beating her head against the washer and dryer; every other month, that man would break another piece of her body or bruise it. Fuck, no one was helping her, so I decided to help her out, and in between me helping her, we fell in love with each other. Don't give me that look right now because I feel I will air out everyone's dirty laundry, and we all know I know everyone's shit. You guys uphold Mike like he's the golden child when, in actual fact, that man is like the devil, and you guys have been enabling him since we were 17. Do you forget the girl he got pregnant? What's her name again. Anastasia. Anastasia was pregnant with his baby, and what did he do when he found out? He beat that poor girl to a pulp and caused her to lose her baby. The poor girl ended up with short-term memory loss and forgot about him beating her, and you guys covered it up and sent him away," my pops tried to interject and stop me, but I had more to say.

"Nah, I'm not finished. What about Gabby, Terrie, Dawn, Tegan, Michelle. What about my ex-girlfriend Stacy-ann, who he stole from me? Fuck Stacy-ann still, to this day, is permanently blind in one eye because of him. All you guys do is cover up what he does, and he thinks he can get anyway with it all; and before you ask, no, me being with Kenya is not payback for Stacy-ann. I genuinely love Kenya with all my heart; I loved her so much that I put a baby in her, she was going to have my 1st son, but because of that arsehole, that will not happen now since she lost the baby," I said with tears running down my face. Every emotion I had came crashing down on me all at once.

My parents sat on the phone in shock, horror, pain, whatever you want to call it, but it was silent for over 10 minutes. No one said a word. All that could be heard was the thumping of my steering wheel being hit repeatedly and my breathing, trying desperately to calm down.

"Jason, look we.."

"Man, forget it 'cause I know you guys ain't gone do shit anyway; you guys are fucked up people, especially you mom, knowing all these women went through with him."

"Now, what a second.."

"I don't want to hear it, I'm gone, but before I go, mom pop's been fucking Aunt Tracie behind your back for the last 2 years, and that baby she had 2 months ago that baby you love so much it's his baby. Also, pop's mom's sleeping with your boss; that's how you got that promotion, by her opening up her legs and sucking dick".

And with that, I hung up the phone and left them spewing in hate. Did I feel bad about letting out their secrets... at this point FUCK NO!

A few days had passed since the whole debacle happened, and I knew I needed to return to work. While looking at my phone, I noticed I had an email from my boss asking me to come in today at 10 a.m. FUCK.

I got dressed and made my way to work. Once I arrived, I could feel everyone's eyes; even the pupils' eyes were on me. Did they know what had happened Friday night?

"Jason, this way, please," said Principal Edwards or, as the students called him, Mr Trunchball.

"Jason, please explain what happened Friday night, please, because for my life, I don't understand what happened, and if I find out that you were in a romantic relationship, then I'm sorry it will not end well for the both of you."

"Well, Trumen, I don't know what to say to you; my brother started the fight over nothing, and then it turned into a massive fight, but when it comes to Kenya... yeah, we are romantically involved."

"I knew it, Jesus, Jason, your brother's wife?"

"Yeah, man, I know."

"Jason, I'm sorry to tell you this, but you know it goes against our policy, and you know I have to fire the both of you for this."

"I thought as much."

"Can you tell Kenya to check her emails as well? I have tried to contact her but have not heard a response."

"And you won't hear one from her right now as she is in a coma."

"A coma!" he shouted with a shocked look.

"Yeah, they ended in a car crash after leaving on Friday."

"Excuse my French but fuck me, is everyone okay, well apart from Kenya?"

"Ummm, hard to say. Mike's fine; he just has a broken arm, but as I said Kenya's in the hospital but she also lost the baby she was carrying."

"Your baby?"

"Yeah, man, I know how this sounds and looks, but it is what it is."

"Off the record, Jason, I consider you a good friend and colleague, but I started to fear for Kenya, especially after the incident that happened in the car park. I started to see many bruises on her, and she would take a lot of time off due to her breaking a bone or something. At first, I did not think anything of it because she is a clumsy person, always bumping into something, but this was something else. I did pull her to one side before and ask if everything was okay, but she just brushed me off. Even the students have complained about how she is and were concerned for her, but she,, likes to brush everything off. Was he, or is he putting his hands on her?"

I hung my head down, neither confirming nor denying his claims, and I guess that's all he needed to know.

"Look, man, not speaking as your boss, well ex-boss, but look after her. That woman is special but is being put through the wars. Protect her at all costs."

I nodded, and with that, I left his office and started packing my stuff. While packing my stuff, I received a phone call from my pops.

"She's awake; I just wanted to let you know. Also, don't bring your ass down here right now."

"Pops, I just.."

"Save it, you've said enough." Instant guilt started to pour in. "But thanks for putting me up on the game." I knew what he was talking about; he was talking about Mom and his boss. "But little nigga how you know about Tracie's baby being mine?"

"The baby got your birthmark and looks like you, plus his name is C.J. At that point, I thought you were just telling on yourself, especially with how attached he is to you."

He chuckled because he knew Clavin Junior looked just like him.

"You're too smart for your own good, you know that."

I chuckled

"Well, like I said, don't come here yet; let the heat die down, and then do you. Also, son, check on your mom; she never knew Tracie's baby being mine too well. Mann, I fucked up a solid friendship, a 30+ friendship," he said, then put the phone down.

Kenya's awake finally. It's time to end this shit and get my women to come home.

Chapter 7

Back in Kenya's hospital room

Bright lights flashed before my eyes, making it extremely difficult for me to focus. I closed my eyes, thinking it would help me adjust my sight, but it never did. I gave it another go, and finally, I was able to see, well, kind of see. My vision was blurry. I could see figures but could not make them out until they started talking.

I blinked my eyes, and I began to focus.

Was I in the hospital? Wait, what the fuck happened? How did I end up here? I had so many questions with no answers. Literally, I was coming up blank.

"Son, she's waking up." I turned my head, and it was Jason's father, Ruban. "Shelia, go call the doctor," he said to his wife. I don't know what it is, but I could feel the tension between them two; I wonder what happened?

I looked to my left, and I could see my husband. OMG, what happened to my husband? Why does he have a broken arm? What the fuck happened. I tried to speak but was unable to. Ruban told me not to try and talk as I had a tube in my mouth, and he told me to wait until the doctor came to take it out.

Sheila came back with a bunch of nurses and doctors who kept telling me to keep still and to take a deep breath in.

"Ahhh, there we go, welcome back, Ms. Kenya; I'm just going to shine this light in your eyes and do some tests just to make sure everything is working correctly. I want you to nod your head if you understand, okay?" I nodded my head. "Okay, do you feel this? How about this? Can you wiggle your toes for me, please? Excellent, that is very good. Right, you will have a bit of a concussion, which is normal due to the trauma of you hitting your head so far. Also, you have a broken arm and a cracked rib. But Kenya, I'm sorry to say the baby did not make it. Unfortunately, there was too much damage and too much bleeding as the placenta had become detached," the doctor said

Baby, what baby? I've not been pregnant in over 2years. What, wait, a baby? I was pregnant, and I lost the baby. I cried for the baby I lost even though I did not know I was pregnant and don't remember ever being pregnant.

I looked at Mike, and he had an angry look on his face like he could kill me. I tried to talk but was unable as my mouth was dry. The doctor gave me some water, and I took some sips of water.

"Doctor, how can I lose a baby when I was never pregnant?"

"Umm, you do know you were pregnant right?"

"No, the last time I was pregnant was 2 years ago."

"Hmm, interesting, Kenya. I'm going to check your eyes again, and I'm going to ask you some questions."

"Okay"

"Right, look here and follow my finger, please, Kenya; you tell me what you have done today, please."

"Well, I finally finished sorting out our new walk-in closet, and I made my husband his favourite dish for lunch."

"Can you tell me what the dish was?"

"Chicken parmesan, he loves that."

"Okay, after you made his lunch, what did you do?"

"I got ready because we were going out for his parent's 7th anniversary at the Radisson Blu Hotel."

I heard a gasp, and it came from Ms. Sheila.

"Kenya, that was 2 years ago."

I gasped

"HAVE I BEEN ASLEEP FOR 2 YEARS? OMG, I WAS PREGNANT. DID SOMEONE ATTACK ME IN MY SLEEP?" I said while panicking.

"Oh god no, Kenya, please calm down. Nothing like that has happened, and you were asleep for a few days. I fear you may have short-term memory loss; not to worry, your memories will return to you, but I can not tell you when that's up to you and your body.

Chapter 8

After over three weeks, I was finally released from the hospital. I was so happy to go home, especially since the hospital food was so disgusting and unseasoned. If you like salt and pepper as a seasoning, then the hospital food is for you, but nahhh, I like my meat, fish, veg, gravy and potatoes well seasoned.

No more doctors trying to prod me, draw blood, and make me do remembering exercises to help me regain my memory. Everything was going great; even my relationship with Mike was going great. He seemed to care about me and my injuries, but an elephant was still in the room.

Me being pregnant

Well, I'm not with child any more. My heart broke just semi-knowing. I once had a life growing inside of me, but due to the accident, the baby had died. I discovered it was a boy I was carrying; I did not know if I should have cried, so I chose to push it at the back of my mind and focus on what was going on.

The fact that my mind was telling me that two years ago was happening right now was mind-boggling. Everything around me confused me; for example, the home Mike brought me to was not the one I remembered. This house had five bedrooms, three and a half bathrooms, two living rooms, a man cave, a huge back garden with a swimming pool and firepit, a massive kitchen with a breakfast bar, a utility room and a four-car garage. Life was perfect for us because the old house was a 2-and-a-half-bedroom home with parking on the street. Yeah, we had moved on up in the world. Well, there was one thing that stayed the same I guess we never had money in the budget to get me a better car. I was still riding around in my beat-up bucket; well, it was not a bucket, it was a 2011 Honda Accord, but still, there was Mike riding around in a new 2014 Audi A3. The only reason I knew what it was was because I had asked him, but when I did, he sounded like he had a lot of animosity towards me. I guess my new car was the car that got wrecked in the accident.

"Why are you looking at me like that?" I asked Mike

"No reason. Are you okay? Do you need me to do something for you?"

"No, I'm okay, thank you."

"Okay, well, I'm off. I got something to sort out."

"Wait, what kind of things? And are you really going to leave me alone right now? You know the doctors told you that I need help with things around the house, plus you have all my medicine."

"You not an invalid, your legs not broken, and your medicine is on the counter, your good."

"I ll might be good, but I still don't want to be alone right now; I'm scared, especially since this is a new house."

"This is not a new house; we have been in here for nearly two years now."

"Yeah, but it's new to me."

"I don't give a.... Look, I got to go. I'll be back later; just don't go nowhere or do any or speak to anyone."

"Speak to anyone who am I.. what do you mean don't speak to anyone?" I was so perplexed by what he was saying. "Mike, where are you going? Explain to me...Mike, Mike," I shouted behind his back, only for him to continue walking out of the house.

Did this man really walk out on me? Yes, yes, he did. What an arsehole

4 hours had passed, and Mike still had not returned; I had managed to take all my tablets on time, but I was very lonely. I had slept thinking by the time I had woken up he would be back, but no such luck.

Ding ding dong

The doorbell went; who's this coming to the house without letting me know I thought to myself.

"Kenya, you're home. I'm so glad you're okay," Jason said while rushing me and giving me a loving hug.

Mwah

Jason's lips had connected to mine. At first, I was surprised, and then I felt a familiar feeling in my heart, and it felt warm and fuzzy until it didn't.

"What the hell do you think you're doing? You know I'm with your brother. I can't believe you just kissed me. Omg, you've made me a cheater. Omg, I've just cheated on my husband," I said, spiralling out of control while pacing up and down. Jason had closed the front door and made his way to me.

"Calm down, Kenya, you're not a cheater, baby."

"Calm down, calm down he says, why would I calm down after what you have done?"

"Baby, please stop this," he said while holding my hands.

"Let go of me and stop calling me baby. I'm your sister-in-law and nothing more," I said while ripping my hands away from his. "Ba..." I gave him a warning look, and he sighed. "Kenya, we have been together for the last nearly 2 years."

Boom!!

My mind was blown. How could this man believe I would even touch him? I'm not saying that in another lifetime, I wouldn't because I would. Have you seen this man? He was so fucking sexy and thuggish without being a thug. I could just jump on him right now and fuck his brains out. Wait, let me stop and stop letting my intrusive thoughts get the better of me.

"The fuck do mean we been together for 2 years? How is that even possible when I've been with Mike?"

"Been with Mike? No, you haven't. Kenya, the baby you lost was mine." Wait, the baby was his. Had I slept with my husband's brother? Everything around me went silent as I was reeling from the information he had given me. I tried to think and see if I could remember anything, but my mind kept coming up blank.

"Kenya, look, I've got proof of what I am saying."

Jason took out his phone and showed me all the pictures of us together and us at the hospital holding a scan picture. I even saw myself pregnant with Jason's hands wrapped around my semi-naked body. What in the actual fuck is going on!!

"Kenya, do you not remember any of this?" I shook my head no.

"I have memory loss, and I don't remember anything in the last 2 years," I said while sitting down on a chair in the living room.

"Memory loss?"

"Yeah, the doctors told us It's due to the accident, which, of course, I don't remember anything to do with that."

Silence filled the air as I could see the sad and confused look on Jason's face.

"Look, Jason, I'm sorry I can't be the woman you ha.."

"Mike caused the car crash."

Wait, Mike did this?

"What do you mean he caused the crash? How do you know this? Wait, were you there? Were you in the other car?"

"Kenya, I was the one who called the ambulance and basically saved your life." Jason. Saved. Me? "I should have never let you leave with him, and none of this would be happening right now."

"I thought Mike saved me."

"No, it was me, Kenya. I understand that you don't remember anything, but trust me, I would never lie to you. When I tell you we were in love, I mean it. I was even pla."

"NIGGA WHAT THE FUCK ARE YOU DOING IN MY HOUSE!"

We both turned around and saw Mike standing there like he was about to explode. He looked like he was foaming at the mouth, like some rabid animal. But all I could think of was when he came back. I never heard the door open at all, and how long had he been standing there.
Mike came charging towards us, and Jason gently moved me to one side because the way Mike was coming at us, he would have knocked me over.

"There was a service announcement saying you were not allowed anywhere by my bitch"

"Man, don't call her a bitch; she's not a fucking dog."

"I can call that hoe whatever I want to call her since she is my wife."

"She not been your wife for 2 years now, Playboy. That's *MY* wife, *MY* heartbeat, *MY* rib standing right there, address her with some respect nigga. You're a little ass boy in a semi-big man's body. Step down, lil nigga, and address me as big dog, the nigga that took everything from you."

And with that, they both clashed; I screamed as the scene in front of me was traumatic to see. Fights flying left and right. At first, Mike was winning by throwing haymakers, but then Jason grabbed him by the legs and body slammed him to the floor and got on top of his body and proceeded to beat the shit out of Mike. Mike was leaking from his nose and mouth, and one of his eyes was closing. To be honest, just looking at him lying there on the ground made my skin crawl.

Jason threw his last punch and got up from Mike. Mike looked dead since he was not moving; I was physically too scared to move. These men had torn through my whole front room. There were broken chairs and vases, and the big screen TV had two massive cracks in it. There was glass all over the floor, and I could see a huge amount of blood on the floor, but nobody was stabbed from what I could tell; I guess when Mike rushed Jason, he fell into the mirror on the wall since that had a huge chunk of glass missing from it.

Jason walked towards me and gently caressed my face, silently asking if I was okay. I nodded to let him know I was fine, but then my face displayed another look.

Fear.

Mike had risen like a phoenix, well, maybe not a phoenix, more like a zombie coming out of their grave. I guess he got his second wind and was ready for two.

Okay, listen, my mind is weird, and when I saw that he got his second wind, all I could hear in my mind was *'round 2 fight'* in a street fighter tone.

Mike rushed into Jason, and they started fighting again. I guess Mike was trying to get me as well, as he pushed me with force into a wall, and I banged my head against it. My head was throbbing with the pain that had just been caused to me, plus with all the screaming I had been doing, I was bound to give myself a massive headache.

While Mike and Jason were rolling around like rabid dogs, I started to clutch my house as my mind was bombarded with images of me and Mike. Mike standing over me, beating me like a dog. Everything from the past 2 years came flooding back like a hurricane.

I REMEMBER EVERYTHING

Before I could even process what was happening, the front door was broken in.

"Police, put your hands up. Hey, you two, stop fighting, or I will shoot back up. I need backup; excuse me, could you stand over here, please?" an officer said.

The officers who broke into my home had managed to separate them and had put them in handcuffs for their own protection. Mike was screaming and yelling like a rabid animal, especially since he tried to attack one of the officers. This man had spit flying out his mouth with his nose and mouth leaking, and one of his eyes was closed, looking like a busted-up pirate.

"Miss, could you tell me what happened here, please? We got a call from one of your neighbours saying they could hear you screaming again,"

"I was screaming, but I was screaming for them two to stop. We were having a family discussion, and things got heated between the two brothers. Nothing more, nothing less."

"Miss, are you sure that's what happened? As we have on file, this property is classed as a red zone due to domestic violence."

"I'm sure officer"

"Okay then," he said, "but miss, if anything else happens, you call us, okay," he said while secretly passing me a card with his name and number on it. "Right, sir, I'm going to

have to ask you to leave as this is not your residence....”
he said while escorting Jason out.

The police had left, and it was just Mike and me. Nothing was said for over 20 minutes; I started to clear away the mess that had been made until I felt a presence behind me. I turned around and was met with a closed fist straight to my face.

And everything turned black.

Chapter 9

Everything started to flood back all at once. Every broken bone, every scar, every bruise, every insult, and every time I lost a baby due to him. IT ALL CAME BACK.
The way I truly felt about him came flooding back as well, and the way I truly felt about Jason came back. Omg, Jason. The way he looked at me when I kept on rejecting him when he was telling me about us. I can't get it out of my mind. I remembered that the doctor told me about losing our baby.

I didn't get a chance to feel sad because I could taste blood coming out of my nose and lips.
"You see what you have caused now, and now you're bleeding; you have no one to blame but yourself."

"But how is this my fault? I never told you to hit me."

I could see the puzzled look on his face, and that's when I realised I had answered him back like I used to do. I realised I had to be quick and think fast on my feet and act like my memory was still gone.

"You hit me, you really hit me. How could you hit me?" I cried, putting on the best act of my life.

"Why would you hit me? I'm your wife, and you love me, so why would you do this to me?"

"Look, I'm sorry, but this situation is your fault; I'm sure I told you not to speak to that man, and now look at my face; look at our home." his face had returned from the puzzled look he displayed to an annoyed look.

"I I I never told him to come here; he just turned up out of nowhere and started to bombard me."

"I can't deal with this. My lip and nose are busted, and my eye is closed, and the other one is closing." Mike started to walk off, "I'm gonna sleep in the guest room tonight; just stay out of my way." With that, he walked upstairs into the guest bedroom and slammed the door.

A few months passed, and my memory was fully restored; the only thing was I was the only one who knew it had been restored. I hid it from everyone; I even hid it from Jason, which killed me to see his struggling face when he would video call me and *try* to get my memory back.

See, there was a reason why I did it. I was biding my time, and I had a plan of escape. Mike kept on hitting me after my memory had returned, and every time he did it, I would pick a weapon and hide it around the house in places I knew he would never look. In all, I had over 20 weapons stashed around the house. In my heart, I knew the next time Mike hit me would be the last time he would ever get to put his hands on me. I know how it sounds; it sounds like I plan on killing him. Well, trust me, I don't. I just need to defend myself. I was tired of it all, and I could feel my own life force slowly slipping away. SLAM

I heard the front door close; it could only be one person coming in at this time. Mike. Mike had been coming in later and later from *work,* or so he said, but his job was not in a pub, so he came home smelling like cheap, watered-down perfume and alcohol. Then I knew he was somewhere else.

I could hear him stamping his heavy feet up the stairs. I bet this man never even took off his shoes after I'd spent 2 hours cleaning these stairs; trust me, the carpet was absolutely nasty. The whole house was so dirty that I gave it a deep clean today. It took me 6 hours to do the whole house, as I still get dizzy spells here and there.

"KENYAAAAA, where you at?" Mike screamed at me.

"I'm in here, Mike."

Mike came barreling into the master bedroom, smelling straight like a brewery. He was stumbling all over the place. Did he drive here drunk?

"It's all your fault; you're the reason she left me; you're the reason it's all falling apart." Mike was babbling some nonsense, which slowly had me racking my brain. Who was this she, and what was my fault?#

"What are you talking about?"

"Bitch don't talk", he said while taking rather large steps towards me. "Why can't you just dieeeeee" Mike shouted while wrapping his hands around my throat.

"AHHHHHHHH!" I screamed.

I was clawing away at his hands, trying to pry them away from my neck. Every time I managed to get his hands away, he would find a way to squeeze harder.
I decided to knee him in his balls, and he came tumbling down while screaming YOU BITCH at me. I ran out of the room and made it to the stairs, or so I thought.

"Where you going bitch? Get over here."

I don't know how or why, but I heard that in Scorpion's voice.
Mike had grabbed me, but with me struggling to get away from him, I tumbled down the stairs along with Mike. I hit my head on the stairs a couple of times but managed to get away from him, so I ran into the front.
Reaching the front room, I was frantically looking for the weapons I had stashed away, but I could not find help. FUCK. Trust me, I am not able to find them when I need them.

"What you are looking for bitch? You're not going to find them, trust me. I found your little hiding places.
"There's nowhere to run to," he said while putting me in a headlock.

I was struggling to breathe, and my vision had become blurry, but I knew I had to fight, so I rammed the back of my head into his face. On impact, he released me, and his nose started to bleed profusely. I scrambled away and made it to the kitchen; Mike was hot on my heels.

"Stay away from me!"

"You think you were smart? I caught on to your little act. I know you got your memory back, you little slut" Mike said while chasing me around the breakfast nook.

Fuck! The jig is up. How and when did he find out?

Mike had caught up to me and managed to backhand me; I flew and landed next to the sink. I could feel blood leaking from my nose and mouth, but I could not let that deter me from my survival. So, I picked up the wet carving knife I was using when I was sorting out dinner. I gripped it and swung towards him, but I missed.

"You little bitch, how dare you" Mike shouted.

I could see murder in his eyes, and I knew it would come down to me or him. I swung again and managed to slice his arm.

"FUCKING BITCH "

Mike managed to grab my arm, and we both started to struggle for the knife. In the process, my cheek got sliced, but I could not focus on the pain.

With all my force, I managed to get a hold of the knife. Mike slipped on the water on the floor from the knife, and

I came down with him as well. As I came down, so did the knife.

Blood ran like water from his belly. Mike, with the strength of 10 men, punched me in the face. My vision became bloody as blood was running down into my eyes; all I saw was red. With the last bit of strength I had left, I picked up the knife, and Mike ran into my knife; he *ran into my knife ten times.*

I could hear the front door banging; my guess it was the police. With all the screaming I was doing, I knew someone had called the police. And I was correct because 5 seconds later I could hear the police.

I let go of the knife and looked over to see Mike lying lifeless with his eyes open. I could see the police but could not hear them since all I could hear in my mind was the lyrics from the film Chicago.

He had it coming, he had it coming
He only had himself to blame
If you'd have been there, if you'd have seen it
I betcha you would have done the same

And with that, I blacked out.

Chapter 10

Kenya is back in the prison hall

Present time

"So yeah, that's how I ended up here; I guess you could say I am a woman scorned, but I'm just a woman who what do the kids say? I'm a woman who got her lick back and then some. As you know, I gave myself up, and I'm serving my time peacefully. Do I regret everything that happened? No, no, I do not, but do I wish I could change things? Yes, I do. I wish I could have gotten out of that marriage and been with my true love; I wish my baby was here; I wish my coma life was my actual life, but sadly, that's not and never going to happen.

The trial became worldwide news, and I had a good defence lawyer, but at the end of the day, I pleaded guilty, which was not news to anyone as I had been saying I was guilty as soon as I got arrested, for Christ's sake.

I still keep in contact with Jason; I get to see him next week, and I can't wait. He's the only form of contact I have with the outside world besides my brother Lance; my mother semi-disowned me for killing *her son-in-law*, and I'm okay with that. This whole ordeal was hard on him, especially when it came to the trial as they tried to drag my name through the mud, but because of my defence and the witnesses coming to my aid and speaking on behalf of me, which was a total surprised me as I thought that only Jason cared for me.

Do you want to know who shocked me as a witness for my side? Ms Sheila. I know I can see your faces; I had the same look as well. She gave evidence of everything that she knew Mike had done to me and gave a WHOLE portfolio on the women before me, which I never knew anything about. That man was a serial beater, a serial abuser, a serial professional dickhead.

In my own way, I feel I got justice for all of them, but mostly myself.

Oh wait, I almost forgot. I also found out Mike had a baby on me, and I know what you're going to say, 'But you were having a baby on him,' and that may be true, but this man had another family on me with the woman he was cheating on me with for three years. They have a five-year-old little girl, I'm not sure what her name is, and they had a little baby who would be around two years old, I think. I only found this out because of the trial, and they dug into EVERYTHING. It turns out the woman he cheated on me with and had a family with was done for embezzlement. That woman tried to take all his money and mine but got caught since she was trying to do it to someone else as well; ain't that a bitch. But yeah, that's my story."

Silence surrounded me, and it made me look at everyone's face and analyse it.

"First of all, thank you for sharing that Kenya."

"Wait, Ms Gates, I just got to say, yo Kenya, that story shocked the fuck out of me, especially since you look like butter wouldn't melt, and you don't look like someone who should be here, but I guess you can't judge a book by its cover," an inmate said

The other inmates were all laughing except one. This inmate had been staring at me like she wanted to kill me all throughout telling this story; I wondered what her issue was.

Ding ding

"Alright, ladies, that's all we have time for; we will pick this back up next week at the same time."
The prison officer Williams came to collect us and bring us all back to our cells.

I reached my cell and sat on my bed, reflecting on everything that had transpired that day. I sat reminiscing on the good times I shared with Mike before everything went bad. Mike was a handsome man and a beautiful soul at first. I choose to remember him that way and not the monster version of him. Do you know who he reminds me of, well, his behaviour? He reminds me of Klaus from Vampire Diaries and Originals, but the only difference is we grew to love Klaus because everything he did was for his family and the people he loved. In Mike's case, I grew to hate and despise him and everything he stood for; he did everything for himself, a selfish bastard. No, let me not talk ill of the dead, rest his soul; after all, I did end it. I pray every day and night, hoping God will forgive me for the crime I committed a sinful act, something I'm not proud of.

I felt something wet hit my hand, and that's when I realised I was crying. I think this was my first time actually crying. I held it all inside and never let it out until now.

I was crying for myself, Jason, my family, Mike's family, and all the women he hurt. But oddly enough, I was also crying for Mike himself. I know, right I'm crying for Mike, of all people. Most of my tears were for all of the babies I had lost, especially for baby Blessing. Blessing is the name I had chosen to call mine and Jason's baby, who never made it. He would have been a blessing to both of us. My baby. My beautiful unborn child, oh, how I loved you from every flutter to every kick. I loved you; every time you made me throw up my food, I loved you through the sleepless nights because you were mine. He would have been the best of both of us. I hope he is up in heaven with the rest of his brothers and sisters looking down on me, smiling as I look up, smiling at them. My beautiful unborn children.

"Hey, so your story time today was interesting, but you missed out on a couple of key facts." I looked up to see who was talking to me, and it was the inmate who kept staring at me like she wanted to kill me.

"You mind taking a step back, please."

"Nah, I can't do that" What the fuck does she mean she can't do that? "See, your story time was cute and all, but you missed some major facts."

"How did I miss facts when it's my life and story? Make that makes sense."

"Let me explain and tell you a little story," she said while stepping back and pacing back and forth in my little room. "See, women like you like to think you are the victim and since a good-looking man came and rescued you from your dull life, you act like you have never done anything to make that man do you the way he did. You laughed at the woman in your story who got sent to jail for stealing from your husband, and now she has to look after two kids by herself. Shit like that is not funny."

"Bitch why are you in my face about this shit? My life has nothing to do with you, so back up and get the fuck out of my room," I shouted.

"Nothing to do with it? BITCH I'M IN HERE BECAUSE OF YOUUUUU" she screamed while swinging a shiv at me. While trying to fight for my life, my mind was trying to think who this woman was and how is she in here because of me.

"BITCH I HATE YOU FOR RUINING MY LIFE, YOU KILLED MY BABY HOE. DIEEEEE BITCH DIEEEEEEE"

"Yo somebody come help; she got a shank; she's gonna kill that woman," shouted an inmate

It was a fight for life and death.

Slash

The bitch managed to slice my arm open, but I could not focus on that. My mission was to get the weapon out of her hands and far away from me. I did not mind boxing it out old school; I got kind of good at it since trying to defend myself against Mike.

"Inmate put the weapon down, requesting back up." Officer Williams said, and about three other officers came to help him. "Take this inmate to the hole and take the other one to the infirmary; she's bleeding a lot."

"BITCH I GOT AIDS AND MY BABY DIED BECAUSE OF YOU, AND NOW YOU GOT THEM TOO," the crazy lady said. It was not until she said she had aids I knew who she was. This bitch was the woman who Mike cheated on me with, and she was robbing him blind. She got found out because she slipped up and got sloppy, and my lawyer found her and found out what she was doing.
BITCH THAT WAS EVELYN!!

Mike's hoe was in here trying to kill me... wait, hold up my arm; it's bleeding; she cut me. Does this mean I have aids now? She would not have said it if it was true; shit, the doctors here need to check me out. FUCK I CAN'T DIE. PLEASE, GOD, DON'T LET THIS BE MY PUNISHMENT FOR TAKING A LIFE.
PLEASE, I'M BEGGING YOU.

The end..... or is it?

Author group on facebook: Kerisha's stories

My starting out babies

1. The blue flower
2. The monster inside
3. The secrets we share

The main books

1. Melanin Queens
2. Melanin Queens pt 2
3. The girl is mine
4. Fighting for my life

Printed in Great Britain
by Amazon

28457665R00046